THE SPIRIT OF KWANZAA: A JOURNEY

BY

KERRY BRACKETT

Dedicated to my family who always supported me, no matter what I decided to do in life. Love you!

Copyright © 2025 Kerry Brackett
All rights reserved

Table of Contents

Chapter 1

The Disconnect

Chapter 2

A Night of Shadows

Chapter 3

The Spirit of Umoja

Chapter 4

Kujichagulia's Challenge

Chapter 5

The Call of Ujima

Chapter 6

Ujamaa's Vision

Chapter 7

Rediscovering Nia

Chapter 8

The Inspiration of Kuumba

Chapter 9

Faith in Imani

Chapter 10

A New Beginning

Books by Kerry Brackett

ABOUT THE AUTHOR

Chapter 1

The Disconnect

The late afternoon sun cast a golden glow over the skyline of Atlanta, but Vanessa Thompson barely noticed as she sat in her high-rise office, immersed in her work. Her startup, TechSphere Innovations, was on the brink of a major breakthrough, and she was determined to see it through. The office was a testament to her success: sleek, modern furniture, state-of-the-art technology, and a view that stretched across the city. Yet, amidst the tangible signs of her achievements, Vanessa felt an intangible void growing inside her.

Vanessa had always been driven. From a young age, she was taught the values of hard work and perseverance by her parents, who had emigrated from the South in search of better opportunities. They instilled in her a deep sense of pride in her African American heritage, celebrating cultural traditions with zeal. But as Vanessa's career took off, those family gatherings and cultural celebrations became infrequent, overshadowed by deadlines and business meetings.

This evening, the office was quiet except for the rhythmic tapping of keyboards and the occasional buzz of a phone. Her team had left hours ago, eager to start their holiday festivities, but Vanessa remained, her mind consumed by the upcoming pitch to a group of influential investors. Securing their backing could elevate TechSphere Innovations to new heights, something she had envisioned since its inception.

As she reviewed the presentation slides one last time, her phone buzzed with a text from her younger brother, Malik. "Hey, sis! Don't forget about the family Kwanzaa dinner tomorrow. Hope you can make it. Love ya!"

Vanessa sighed, feeling a pang of guilt. The annual Kwanzaa dinner was a cherished tradition, a time when her family gathered to reflect on the seven principles that guided their lives. But each year, Vanessa found it harder to attend, her obligations pulling her in different directions.

"I'll try, Malik," she texted back, though she knew her chances of attending were slim.

The clock ticked toward evening, and as the city lights began to twinkle, Vanessa leaned back in her chair, trying to shake off the fatigue. Her eyes drifted to a photograph on her desk: a family portrait taken years ago during a Kwanzaa celebration. Everyone was smiling, dressed in vibrant traditional attire, the warmth and love almost palpable.

Just as she was about to refocus on her work, the power suddenly flickered and went out, plunging the office into darkness. Vanessa's heart skipped a beat. She stood up, her eyes slowly adjusting to the dim afterglow of the setting sun outside. The silence was thick, interrupted only by the distant hum of the city below.

Fumbling for her phone, Vanessa turned on the flashlight and made her way to the hallway. The emergency lights had kicked in, casting eerie shadows along the walls. She glanced around, expecting to see someone from the building's maintenance team, but the corridor was empty.

As she debated whether to call security, a soft, rhythmic drumming resonated through the air, followed by a faint chanting. The sound was both foreign and familiar, stirring something deep within her. Vanessa's pulse quickened. She knew she must be imagining things, the stress of work playing tricks on her mind.

Shaking her head to dispel the unease, Vanessa returned to her office, determined to finish her preparations despite the power outage. But the drumming continued, persistent and haunting, as if calling to her from another time and place.

Sitting alone in the dim light, Vanessa couldn't shake the feeling that something extraordinary was about to unfold—something that would challenge her perceptions and reconnect her with a part of herself she had long forgotten.

Chapter 2

A Night of Shadows

Vanessa sat motionless in her darkened office, the only light coming from her phone's flashlight, which cast long, wavering shadows across the walls. The rhythmic drumming and chanting persisted, growing slightly louder, more insistent. Each beat seemed to resonate within her, stirring memories she couldn't quite grasp.

She stood up, her curiosity piqued despite the eerie circumstances. Vanessa had read about similar sounds in stories her grandmother used to tell—tales of ancestral spirits and the power of tradition. But those were just stories, she reminded herself, passed down through generations to teach and guide. This was reality, an office building in the heart of Atlanta, not some mystical realm.

Still, the sound was undeniable.

Venturing out into the hallway again, Vanessa called out, hoping for a rational explanation. "Hello? Is anyone there?" Her voice echoed back at her, the emptiness of the building amplifying her unease.

The emergency lights flickered intermittently, casting an unsettling glow over the deserted corridor. Vanessa's footsteps echoed softly as she moved toward the source of the sound, her heart pounding with each step. She reached the end of the hallway, where a stairwell led up to the rooftop. The drumming was clearer now, emanating from above, urging her to follow.

With a deep breath, Vanessa ascended the stairs, each step a mix of apprehension and anticipation. The chanting was distinct now, words she couldn't understand but felt compelled to follow. Reaching the top, she hesitated before pushing open the heavy metal door that led to the rooftop.

The city stretched out before her, a sea of lights under the dark sky. The cold night air was a sharp contrast to the warmth inside the building. Vanessa wrapped her arms around herself, scanning the empty rooftop. There was no one there, just the wind and the distant sounds of the city below.

Yet the drumming continued, now seeming to come from within her own mind, a haunting melody that evoked a deep sense of connection and longing. Vanessa closed her eyes, letting the sound envelop her, feeling an inexplicable pull toward something greater than herself.

Suddenly, the drumming ceased, replaced by an intense silence. Vanessa opened her eyes, startled to find she was no longer alone. Standing before her was a figure, ethereal and shimmering as if made of moonlight. The figure was dressed in traditional African attire, rich fabrics that seemed to ripple with energy.

Vanessa gasped, instinctively stepping back, her mind racing to comprehend the impossible. The figure regarded her with kind, yet penetrating eyes, and though its lips never moved, Vanessa heard a voice—gentle yet firm, resonating within her.

"Fear not, child of the diaspora," the voice intoned. "You have been chosen to embark on a journey of remembrance and renewal."

Vanessa blinked, struggling to find her voice. "Who… what are you?" she finally managed, her voice trembling with disbelief.

The figure smiled, a warmth that melted some of her apprehension. "I am Umoja, the spirit of unity. I come to remind you of the ties that bind you to your ancestors, your family, and your community."

Vanessa's mind spun with questions, but before she could ask them, Umoja gestured toward the city below, and the rooftop transformed. Vanessa found herself standing in a vibrant scene from the past—a bustling village filled with laughter and song, families gathered in celebration, their faces glowing with joy and unity.

She watched, mesmerized, as the scene unfolded around her, a tapestry of lives intertwined by shared history and purpose. Vanessa felt a sense of belonging, a connection that transcended time and space. In that moment, she understood that her heritage was not just a part of her past, but a living, breathing force within her.

As the vision faded, Vanessa was back on the rooftop, the city lights twinkling in the distance. Umoja's presence lingered, a comforting reminder of the journey she was about to undertake. The spirit's voice echoed softly in her mind, "Remember, Vanessa. Remember who you are and where you come from."

With those words, Umoja vanished, leaving Vanessa alone under the vast expanse of the night sky. She stood there for a moment, the cold air bracing against her skin, her heart filled with a new resolve. Vanessa knew that this night marked the beginning of an extraordinary journey—one that would lead her back to her roots and reshape her future.

Chapter 3

The Spirit of Umoja

The following morning, Vanessa awoke with a lingering sense of awe and wonder. The events of the previous night hovered at the edge of her consciousness, vivid yet surreal. As she got ready for the day, her mind replayed the vision shown to her by the spirit of Umoja—the vibrant village, the feeling of unity, and the profound connection to her heritage. It was as if a veil had been lifted, revealing a world rich with meaning and history that she had long neglected.

At the breakfast table, Vanessa glanced at her phone, scrolling through a series of work emails and meeting reminders. Yet, the usual urgency she felt was now tempered by the memory of Umoja's visit. She paused, her finger hovering over Malik's text from the previous evening about the Kwanzaa dinner. After a moment of hesitation, she replied, "I'm coming tonight. Wouldn't miss it for the world."

Determined to make time for her family and cultural roots, Vanessa decided to handle her work with a renewed sense of balance. She spent the morning at her office, meeting with her team and making final preparations for the upcoming investor pitch. However, the spirit's message stayed with her, influencing her decisions and interactions in subtle but significant ways.

By the afternoon, Vanessa felt a strange anticipation building inside her. She couldn't shake the feeling that her experience with Umoja was only the beginning. As the workday came to a close, she grabbed her coat and left the office early, eager to reconnect with her family and immerse herself in the Kwanzaa celebration.

Arriving at her parents' home, Vanessa was greeted by the warm, familiar smell of spices and home-cooked food. The house was bustling with activity, filled with laughter and the joyful sounds of her family preparing for the evening's festivities. Vanessa felt a rush of nostalgia as she stepped inside, her heart swelling with affection for the people she held dear.

Her mother, Grace, was in the kitchen, overseeing the preparation of the traditional feast. She looked up with a surprised smile as Vanessa entered. "Well, look who finally decided to join us!" Grace teased, wrapping her daughter in a warm hug. "We've missed you, Vanessa."

Vanessa returned the embrace, feeling a wave of gratitude wash over her. "I've missed you too, Mom. I'm really glad to be here."

As the evening unfolded, Vanessa found herself fully engaged in the celebration. The living room was adorned with colorful Kwanzaa decorations, and the table was set with a beautiful kinara at its center, each candle representing one of the seven principles. Vanessa listened as her father, James, spoke about Umoja, the principle of unity, sharing stories of their ancestors and the importance of community bonds.

Vanessa felt a newfound appreciation for these traditions, seeing them not just as rituals, but as a living connection to her past and a guide for her future. As her family gathered around the table to light the first candle, Vanessa felt a sense of peace and belonging that she hadn't experienced in years.

Later, as the evening wound down, Malik pulled Vanessa aside. "I'm really glad you made it, sis," he said, his eyes reflecting the same warmth and unity that Umoja had shown her. "I know things have been busy for you, but you're always a part of this family, no matter what."

Vanessa nodded, feeling the truth of his words resonate within her. "I know, and I'm sorry I've been so distant. I've realized how important it is to stay connected to where we come from. Last night, I… I had an experience that reminded me of that."

Malik raised an eyebrow, intrigued. "An experience? You mean with work?"

Vanessa hesitated, unsure of how to explain the encounter with Umoja. "Not exactly. It's hard to explain, but it's made me see things differently. I feel like I'm on a journey to reconnect with my roots, and I want to make more time for family and our traditions."

Malik smiled, giving her a supportive nod. "That sounds amazing, Vanessa. Whatever it is, I'm here for you."

As Vanessa drove home that night, the city lights blurring past her windows, she reflected on the day's events. The sense of unity she had felt with her family was a powerful reminder of the connections that defined her identity. Her encounter with Umoja had opened her eyes to the importance of embracing her heritage, and she knew there would be more to learn on this journey.

The road ahead was uncertain, but Vanessa felt ready to face it, guided by the wisdom of the past and the support of her family. She was determined to honor her roots and integrate the principles of Kwanzaa into her life, both personally and professionally. As she pulled into her driveway, she glanced up at the night sky, wondering what other spirits might be waiting to guide her on her path of discovery and renewal.

Chapter 4

Kujichagulia's Challenge

The morning after the Kwanzaa dinner, Vanessa awoke with a renewed sense of purpose. The memories of the previous night lingered in her mind, particularly the warmth and unity she felt with her family. Yet, she also sensed there was more to uncover, more to understand about her identity and heritage. The encounter with Umoja had opened a door, and Vanessa was ready to step through it.

After a day of meetings and planning sessions at the office, Vanessa returned home, feeling the weight of her responsibilities but also a growing curiosity about what lay ahead. As evening descended, she settled into her favorite armchair, a cup of herbal tea in hand. Her apartment was quiet, the only sound the gentle hum of the city outside.

As she relaxed, her thoughts drifted to the Kwanzaa principle of Kujichagulia—self-determination. She had always prided herself on being self-reliant, on charting her own course in life. But the more she reflected, the more she realized that her definition of self-determination had been narrowly focused on career success. There was a deeper layer she hadn't yet explored.

As if responding to her thoughts, the room grew colder, the temperature dropping noticeably. Vanessa shivered, wrapping her arms around herself as a faint glow appeared in the corner of the room. The glow intensified, coalescing into the figure of a woman, regal and commanding, with features that suggested both wisdom and strength.

Vanessa's breath caught in her throat. The apparition was both beautiful and intimidating, her presence filling the room with an air of authority. The woman wore a traditional African head wrap and robe, her eyes shining with an inner light.

"Do not be afraid, Vanessa," the spirit spoke, her voice resonant and clear. "I am Kujichagulia, the spirit of self-determination. I come to guide you in understanding your true self and your purpose."

Vanessa nodded, her initial surprise giving way to a deep curiosity and respect. "I'm ready to learn," she said, her voice steady despite the surreal circumstances.

Kujichagulia extended her hand, and Vanessa felt a gentle pull, as if she were being drawn into another world. The room around her dissolved, replaced by a vivid scene from her childhood—a small community center where she had spent countless afternoons participating in cultural workshops and activities.

Vanessa watched as her younger self, perhaps ten years old, sat in a circle with other children, listening intently to an elder share stories of African kings and queens, inventors, and leaders. The elder's voice was rich with passion, painting pictures of resilience and brilliance that captured the imagination of the young Vanessa.

Kujichagulia gestured toward the scene. "Remember the dreams you had then, the aspirations that were fueled by these stories of greatness. You were inspired to be more than just a successful businesswoman. You wanted to make a difference, to honor your heritage through your achievements."

Vanessa felt a pang of nostalgia and recognition, recalling the dreams she had harbored as a child. She had wanted to create something meaningful, something that would uplift her community and celebrate her culture.

The scene shifted, and Vanessa found herself in her college dorm room, poring over books and articles about African American history and technology. She remembered those days vividly—her desire to blend her passion for tech with her cultural heritage, to innovate in a way that would empower others.

Kujichagulia's voice gently intruded upon her thoughts. "Your journey of self-determination is not just about personal success. It is about defining who you are in a way that honors your roots and contributes to the world. It is about aligning your actions with your true purpose."

Vanessa nodded, absorbing the spirit's words. She realized how much she had drifted from those early aspirations, caught up in the corporate world and the pursuit of financial success. Her startup, though successful, had become more about profit margins than the values she once held dear.

As the vision faded, Vanessa found herself back in her apartment, the room warmed once more by the spirit's presence. Kujichagulia regarded her with a serene smile. "Remember, Vanessa, self-determination is a journey. It requires you to look within, to understand who you are beyond your titles and achievements. It is a call to live authentically and to inspire others to do the same."

With those final words, Kujichagulia's form began to dissolve, leaving Vanessa alone in the quiet of her apartment. Yet, the spirit's message lingered, echoing in her mind and heart. Vanessa felt a newfound clarity about her path forward—a desire to realign her business and personal life with the values she held dear.

She resolved to revisit her original vision for TechSphere Innovations, to find ways to integrate cultural empowerment into her work. The journey would not be easy, but Vanessa felt ready to embrace it, guided by the principles of self-determination and the lessons from her past.

With a deep breath, Vanessa glanced at the kinara she had placed on her mantle. She whispered a silent promise to herself and her ancestors to honor the spirit of Kujichagulia and to walk boldly into a future defined by her true self.

Chapter 5

The Call of Ujima

The days following Vanessa's encounter with Kujichagulia were filled with contemplation and renewed focus. She felt invigorated by the insights she had gained, more aware than ever of the importance of aligning her ambitions with her deeper values. Yet, she sensed that her journey was far from over. There were more principles to explore—more lessons to learn.

One evening, Vanessa found herself drawn to the quiet refuge of a local community park, a place where she often went to think and reflect. The park was a serene oasis amidst the urban sprawl of Atlanta, its paths lined with towering oaks and benches that invited contemplation. As she walked along the winding trails, Vanessa considered how she might integrate the principle of Kujichagulia into her work and life.

The sun dipped below the horizon, casting a warm glow across the landscape. Vanessa sat down on a bench, her thoughts drifting to the third principle of Kwanzaa: Ujima, or collective work and responsibility. She realized that while she had focused heavily on personal achievement, she had overlooked the broader impact she could have on her community.

As if in response to her thoughts, a gentle breeze stirred the leaves around her, carrying with it a soft, rhythmic melody. Vanessa felt a familiar tingling sensation, a subtle shift in the air that heralded another supernatural encounter. She looked up, and before her stood a tall, imposing figure, emanating a quiet strength and wisdom.

The figure was a man, his presence commanding yet comforting. He wore a traditional African tunic, and his eyes held a depth that spoke of generations of knowledge and experience. Vanessa felt a sense of calm wash over her as she met his gaze.

"I am Ujima," the spirit introduced, his voice resonant and soothing. "I come to remind you of the power and responsibility of working together for the common good."

Vanessa nodded, eager to learn from this new guide. "I've been so focused on my own goals," she admitted. "I want to do more for my community, but I'm not sure where to start."

Ujima smiled, gesturing for her to rise. "Come, let me show you the strength of collective effort."

With a wave of his hand, the park transformed into a vibrant scene of community activity. Vanessa found herself standing in the middle of a bustling neighborhood event, where people of all ages and backgrounds worked together to improve their surroundings. Some painted murals on walls, others planted flowers in a community garden, while a group of children ran joyfully, playing games that echoed with laughter.

Vanessa watched as a team of volunteers organized a food drive, distributing groceries to families in need. The air buzzed with camaraderie and shared purpose, each person contributing their skills and time for the benefit of all. She was struck by the power of unity, the tangible impact that collective work could have on creating a thriving, supportive community.

"These people have found strength in each other," Ujima explained, his voice carrying the weight of truth. "They understand that by working together, they can overcome challenges and create opportunities for everyone."

As Vanessa observed, she noticed familiar faces among the volunteers—colleagues from her company, neighbors, and even old friends she hadn't seen in years. The realization hit her that she was already part of a network capable of making significant change, if only she embraced the responsibility of leadership and collaboration.

The scene shifted again, and Vanessa found herself in a community center, where local entrepreneurs shared ideas and resources. They discussed projects that lifted up their neighborhood, from educational programs to small business initiatives. Vanessa felt a spark of inspiration, recognizing how her skills and resources could contribute to this thriving ecosystem.

Ujima turned to her, his expression earnest. "Vanessa, you have the ability to be a catalyst for change. By fostering a spirit of collective work and responsibility within your business, you can empower others and build a legacy that goes beyond individual success."

The vision faded, returning Vanessa to the quiet park, the spirit of Ujima still by her side. She felt a profound shift within her, a commitment to integrate Ujima's teachings into her life and work.

"Thank you," Vanessa said, her voice filled with gratitude. "I see now that my success is intertwined with the well-being of my community. I want to help create opportunities and build something meaningful together."

Ujima nodded, his smile warm and encouraging. "Remember, Vanessa, the strength of a community lies in its ability to work as one. Embrace this principle, and you will find fulfillment not just in what you achieve, but in the lives you touch."

With those words, Ujima began to dissolve into the evening air, leaving Vanessa with a renewed sense of purpose. She sat in the park for a while longer, reflecting on the insights she had gained and the path she now felt ready to pursue.

As she made her way home, Vanessa's mind buzzed with ideas. She envisioned new initiatives within TechSphere Innovations that could support local entrepreneurship, educational programs, and community partnerships. She felt a deep sense of excitement, knowing that this was just the beginning of a journey that would not only transform her company but also lift her community.

Vanessa arrived at her apartment with a plan forming in her mind. She was ready to embrace Ujima, to champion collective work and responsibility, and to lead with a vision that honored her heritage and empowered those around her.

Chapter 6

Ujamaa's Vision

The realization that her success was intertwined with the well-being of her community had ignited a new passion within Vanessa. She was eager to transform her business into a platform that not only thrived economically but also supported and empowered others. The principle of Ujima had opened her eyes to the power of collective work, and now she was ready to embrace Ujamaa, the principle of cooperative economics.

Vanessa spent the following days researching community-based economic models and brainstorming ways to integrate these ideas into TechSphere Innovations. She reached out to local business leaders and community organizers, eager to understand their needs and explore potential collaborations. The more she learned, the more she saw the potential for her company to be a force for positive change.

One evening, as Vanessa sat at her dining table surrounded by notes and sketches, she felt the now-familiar sensation of a shift in the air. The room seemed to grow warmer, the shadows softening as a gentle glow filled the space. Vanessa looked up, and there stood a figure radiating warmth and kindness.

The spirit was a woman, her presence vibrant and comforting. She wore a richly patterned kente cloth, and her eyes sparkled with intelligence and compassion. Vanessa felt an immediate connection, as if she were in the company of an old friend.

"Greetings, Vanessa," the spirit said, her voice melodic and reassuring. "I am Ujamaa, the spirit of cooperative economics. I come to guide you in creating prosperity that is shared and sustainable."

Vanessa smiled, her heart swelling with anticipation. "I've been thinking a lot about how to support my community through my business," she confessed. "I want to make a real difference."

Ujamaa nodded, her expression one of approval. "The journey you are on is one of great potential. Let me show you the power of shared wealth and collective prosperity."

With a graceful motion, Ujamaa gestured around her, and the room transformed into a bustling marketplace. Vanessa found herself standing amidst stalls brimming with goods, where vendors greeted customers with warm smiles. The air was alive with the sounds of lively exchanges, laughter, and the rich aroma of spices and food.

"This is a place where commerce thrives through collaboration," Ujamaa explained, leading Vanessa through the vibrant scene. "Here, businesses work together, supporting each other and reinvesting in their community."

Vanessa watched as vendors traded resources, shared knowledge, and promoted each other's products. The marketplace was a hub of activity, where everyone benefited from the success of others. She saw small businesses pooling their resources to purchase supplies in bulk, lowering costs and increasing profits for all involved. Entrepreneurs mentored young people, passing on skills and creating opportunities for the next generation.

The atmosphere was one of mutual respect and shared goals. Vanessa felt inspired by the sight of a community that understood the value of cooperative economics. She realized that by fostering such an environment within her own company and the broader community, she could contribute to a cycle of growth and empowerment.

Ujamaa turned to Vanessa, her eyes filled with wisdom. "Prosperity is most powerful when it benefits many, not just a few. By embracing cooperative economics, you can create a legacy of opportunity and resilience."

Vanessa nodded, feeling the truth of Ujamaa's words resonate within her. She thought about her business, about the potential partnerships she could forge and the initiatives she could launch to support local entrepreneurs and community projects. She envisioned TechSphere Innovations not just as a tech company, but as a catalyst for economic empowerment.

The scene shifted once more, and Vanessa found herself in a modern co-working space, where creative minds gathered to collaborate and innovate. The energy in the room was electric, a testament to what could be achieved when people pooled their talents and resources.

Vanessa saw herself among them, facilitating connections, providing resources, and nurturing ideas that could transform lives. She felt a surge of excitement, imagining the possibilities that lay ahead.

As the vision faded, Vanessa was back in her apartment, Ujamaa's presence still a comforting glow beside her. The spirit's message had ignited a fire within her—a determination to integrate the principles of cooperative economics into her business model and community outreach.

"Thank you, Ujamaa," Vanessa said, her voice filled with gratitude and resolve. "I understand now how important it is to build a business that uplifts others and creates shared prosperity. I'm ready to take action."

Ujamaa smiled, her expression one of encouragement. "Remember, Vanessa, true success is measured not by what you gain, but by what you give. Embrace this principle, and you will create a legacy that endures."

With those words, Ujamaa's form began to dissolve, leaving Vanessa with a sense of purpose and vision. She sat in the warm glow of her apartment, her mind racing with ideas and plans for the future.

Vanessa knew that the journey ahead would require dedication and collaboration, but she felt ready to embrace the challenge. She was determined to transform TechSphere Innovations into a beacon of cooperative economics, where success was shared and prosperity uplifted all.

As she prepared for bed, Vanessa felt a profound sense of peace and excitement. She was on a path that honored her heritage, empowered her community, and fulfilled her deepest aspirations. With Ujamaa's guidance, she was ready to create a future defined by unity, collaboration, and shared success.

Chapter 7

Rediscovering Nia

The commitment to cooperative economics and collective prosperity had sparked a transformative change in Vanessa's perspective. Yet, as she moved forward in her journey, she knew there was more to uncover—more to align with her personal and professional endeavors. She had embraced Umoja, Kujichagulia, Ujima, and Ujamaa, but she felt the call to delve deeper into the principle of Nia: purpose.

Vanessa spent the following days reflecting on her life's purpose, contemplating how she could channel her talents and resources to make a meaningful impact. She pondered the legacy she wanted to leave behind, not just as an entrepreneur but as a member of her community and a custodian of her cultural heritage.

One evening, as Vanessa sat on her balcony overlooking the Atlanta skyline, the cool night air wrapped around her like a comforting embrace. She gazed at the stars, their quiet brilliance reminding her of the infinite possibilities before her. It was in this quiet moment of contemplation that she felt the familiar shift in the atmosphere—a gentle, inviting presence that seemed to reach out and touch her soul.

Turning, Vanessa saw a figure emerge from the shadows, bathed in a soft, ethereal light. The spirit was a man, dignified and serene, his eyes reflecting the depth of countless stories and forgotten dreams. He wore a traditional agbada, its intricate patterns shimmering with an otherworldly glow.

"Good evening, Vanessa," the spirit greeted, his voice a soothing balm that washed over her. "I am Nia, the spirit of purpose. I come to guide you in aligning your actions with the deeper meaning of your life."

Vanessa felt a sense of calm and assurance in Nia's presence. "I've been thinking a lot about my purpose," she confessed. "I want my work and my life to reflect something greater, something that truly matters."

Nia nodded, his expression one of understanding. "Purpose is the compass that guides us through life. It anchors us to our core values and connects us to the broader tapestry of existence."

With a gentle sweep of his hand, Nia transformed the balcony into a vibrant scene from Vanessa's past—a bustling community center where she had volunteered as a teenager. Vanessa watched as her younger self helped organize educational workshops for local children, her face alight with passion and dedication.

"This is where you first discovered your desire to empower others," Nia explained, gesturing toward the scene. "You wanted to create opportunities and inspire hope, to use your skills to uplift those around you."

Vanessa felt a pang of nostalgia and recognition. She remembered the joy of those early days, the sense of fulfillment that came from making a difference in her community. It was a feeling she had lost touch with in her pursuit of corporate success.

The scene shifted, and Vanessa found herself standing in a classroom filled with eager faces, young students ready to learn and explore. She watched as a teacher guided them through a lesson on technology and innovation, their eyes wide with wonder and curiosity.

"This is the legacy you can leave," Nia said, his voice filled with conviction. "By aligning your talents with your purpose, you can inspire and educate, creating a foundation for future generations to build upon."

Vanessa felt a surge of inspiration as she realized the potential impact of her work. She imagined TechSphere Innovations as more than just a tech company—it could be a platform for empowerment, a resource for education, and a beacon of hope for aspiring innovators.

As the vision faded, Vanessa found herself back on her balcony, the city lights twinkling in the distance. Nia's presence was a comforting glow beside her, his message resonating deep within her heart.

"I understand now," Vanessa said, her voice filled with gratitude and determination. "My purpose is to use my skills and resources to empower others, to create opportunities that reflect the values of my heritage and community."

Nia smiled, his expression one of encouragement. "Remember, Vanessa, purpose is a journey, not a destination. It evolves as you grow and learn, guiding you toward a life of meaning and fulfillment."

With those words, Nia's form began to dissolve, leaving Vanessa with a profound sense of clarity and direction. She sat on the balcony for a while longer, her mind racing with ideas and plans for the future.

Vanessa knew that the journey ahead would require dedication and vision, but she felt ready to embrace the challenge. She was determined to transform TechSphere Innovations into a platform that honored her purpose and empowered others.

As she prepared for bed, Vanessa felt a profound sense of peace and excitement. She was on a path that honored her heritage, fulfilled her deepest aspirations, and created a legacy of opportunity and empowerment. With Nia's guidance, she was ready to embrace a future defined by purpose and meaning.

Chapter 8

The Inspiration of Kuumba

Vanessa's journey thus far had been transformative, guiding her through the principles of unity, self-determination, collective work, cooperative economics, and purpose. Each spirit had offered her invaluable insights, but Vanessa knew there was more to discover. She felt the anticipation of another encounter, a pull toward creativity and innovation that had always been at the heart of her endeavors.

Kuumba, the principle of creativity, was next. Vanessa spent her days nurturing new ideas and exploring ways to infuse her business with cultural richness and innovation. She envisioned projects that celebrated African American culture through technology, blending her passion for tech with her ancestral heritage. Yet, she yearned for a spark, an inspiration that would elevate her vision to new heights.

One evening, Vanessa decided to visit a local art exhibition that celebrated African American artists and their contributions to the cultural tapestry of the city. The gallery buzzed with energy and creativity, each piece a testament to the power of imagination and expression. As she wandered through the exhibits, Vanessa felt a deep connection to the artists' work, their stories resonating with her own journey of self-discovery and empowerment.

As she paused before a vibrant mural depicting scenes of African folklore intertwined with modern urban life, Vanessa felt a shift in the air—a gentle breeze that whispered of change and inspiration. Turning, she saw a figure emerge from the shadows, a radiant presence that filled the gallery with warmth and light.

The spirit was a woman, her attire a kaleidoscope of colors that seemed to shimmer and dance with every movement. Her eyes sparkled with mischief and wisdom, and her smile was infectious, inviting Vanessa into a world of boundless creativity.

"Hello, Vanessa," the spirit greeted, her voice a melodious harmony that enveloped the room. "I am Kuumba, the spirit of creativity. I come to ignite the spark of innovation within you."

Vanessa felt an immediate kinship with Kuumba, her heart lifting with excitement. "I've been searching for ways to blend my work with my heritage," she admitted. "I want to create something that celebrates our culture and inspires others."

Kuumba nodded, her expression one of understanding and encouragement. "Creativity is the bridge between the past and the future. It allows us to honor our roots while forging new paths. Let me show you how you can harness this power."

With a wave of her hand, Kuumba transformed the gallery into a living canvas, each piece of art coming to life in a symphony of color and motion. Vanessa watched in awe as the scenes unfolded around her, each one a story of resilience, innovation, and cultural pride.

The mural before her expanded, revealing a bustling cityscape where technology and tradition coexisted in harmony. Vanessa saw herself walking through the streets, engaging with communities and fostering projects that celebrated cultural heritage through modern innovation. She imagined interactive installations that told stories of African American pioneers in technology, virtual reality experiences that transported users to pivotal moments in history, and educational programs that empowered young people to explore their creative potential.

"This is the legacy you can create," Kuumba explained, her voice a gentle guide. "By infusing your work with creativity, you can inspire others to see the beauty and potential in their own stories."

Vanessa felt a surge of inspiration as she envisioned TechSphere Innovations as a hub of cultural creativity—a place where technology and heritage intersected to create meaningful experiences. She imagined partnerships with artists, educators, and community leaders, collaborating on projects that uplifted and celebrated African American culture.

As the vision faded, Vanessa found herself back in the gallery, the spirit of Kuumba still by her side. Her heart was full of ideas and possibilities, each one a testament to the power of creativity and innovation.

"Thank you, Kuumba," Vanessa said, her voice filled with gratitude and determination. "I understand now how creativity can elevate my work and honor my heritage. I'm ready to bring these ideas to life."

Kuumba smiled, her eyes twinkling with joy. "Remember, Vanessa, creativity is limitless. It is a gift that grows as you nurture it. Embrace this principle, and you will inspire others to do the same."

With those words, Kuumba's form began to dissolve, leaving Vanessa with a renewed sense of purpose and vision. She stood in the gallery for a while longer, her mind racing with ideas and plans for the future.

Vanessa knew that the journey ahead would require courage and innovation, but she felt ready to embrace the challenge. She was determined to transform TechSphere Innovations into a beacon of creativity and cultural celebration, where technology served as a canvas for storytelling and empowerment.

As she left the gallery, Vanessa felt a profound sense of peace and excitement. She was on a path that honored her heritage, fulfilled her deepest aspirations, and inspired others to explore their creative potential. With Kuumba's guidance, she was ready to embrace a future defined by innovation and cultural pride.

Chapter 9

Faith in Imani

The journey through the principles of Kwanzaa had been transformative for Vanessa. Each encounter had deepened her understanding of her heritage, awakened her purpose, and inspired her creativity. However, as she approached the final principle, Vanessa felt a lingering uncertainty about the path she was forging. She realized that embracing these changes required not only vision and commitment but also faith—faith in herself, her community, and the journey ahead.

Imani, the principle of faith, was the final guide she needed to meet. Faith had always been a quiet force in Vanessa's life, one that she had often taken for granted amidst the chaos of her career. Now, she understood its vital role in sustaining her through challenges and uncertainties.

One quiet evening, Vanessa found herself at her grandmother's house—a place filled with cherished memories and the comforting scent of home. The walls were adorned with family photographs, each one a testament to the strength and resilience of her ancestors. Her grandmother, a woman of deep faith and wisdom, had always been a guiding light in Vanessa's life.

As Vanessa sat in the cozy living room, sipping tea and reflecting on her journey, she felt the now-familiar shift in the atmosphere. The room seemed to glow with a gentle light, and the comforting presence of Imani filled the space.

The spirit appeared as an elder, her face lined with the wisdom of countless lifetimes. Her eyes were warm and knowing, and her presence exuded a calm assurance that wrapped around Vanessa like a protective embrace.

"Good evening, Vanessa," Imani said, her voice a soothing melody that resonated deeply. "I am Imani, the spirit of faith. I come to strengthen your belief in the path you are walking."

Vanessa felt a deep sense of peace in Imani's presence. "I've learned so much on this journey," she confessed, "but I sometimes doubt my ability to bring these visions to life. It feels overwhelming."

Imani nodded, her expression one of understanding and compassion. "Faith is the foundation that supports you when the way forward is uncertain. It is the light that guides you through the darkness, the strength that sustains you in times of doubt."

With a serene gesture, Imani transformed the room into a tapestry of Vanessa's life, each thread a moment of triumph and challenge. Vanessa saw herself as a child, learning the stories of her ancestors. She saw her early days of entrepreneurship, filled with passion and determination, and the moments of doubt that had tested her resolve.

Imani guided her through these memories, highlighting the moments where faith had quietly sustained her—her grandmother's prayers, the support of her family, and the unwavering belief in her potential.

"This is the faith that has carried you," Imani explained, her voice a gentle reassurance. "It is woven into the fabric of your being, a testament to the strength of those who came before you."

Vanessa watched as the scene shifted to her future, a vision of what could be if she embraced faith as a guiding force. She saw TechSphere Innovations flourishing, a company that not only thrived economically but also uplifted and empowered others. She saw herself leading with confidence, her work infused with the principles she had embraced.

The vision filled her with hope and determination, a reminder that faith was not just a belief but an action—a commitment to trust in herself and the journey.

As the vision faded, Vanessa found herself back in her grandmother's living room, Imani still by her side. The spirit's presence was a comforting reminder of the strength and resilience that faith could provide.

"Thank you, Imani," Vanessa said, her voice filled with gratitude and resolve. "I understand now that faith is the strength I need to move forward, to trust in the vision and the journey."

Imani smiled, her eyes shining with encouragement. "Remember, Vanessa, faith is the bridge between where you are and where you want to be. It is the anchor that holds you steady and the wings that lift you higher."

With those words, Imani's form began to dissolve, leaving Vanessa with a profound sense of peace and purpose. She sat in the quiet of her grandmother's house, her heart filled with gratitude for the journey she had undertaken and the lessons she had learned.

Vanessa knew that the path ahead would require faith and determination, but she felt ready to embrace the challenge. She was determined to lead with vision and purpose, to honor her heritage and inspire others to do the same.

As she prepared to leave, Vanessa took a moment to reflect on the journey she had undertaken. She felt the presence of each spirit, their teachings woven into the fabric of her being. With faith as her guide, Vanessa was ready to embrace the future, a future defined by purpose, creativity, and community.

With a deep breath and a heart full of hope, Vanessa stepped into the night, the stars above a reminder of the infinite possibilities before her. With Imani's guidance, she was ready to embrace a future defined by faith and fulfillment.

Chapter 10

A New Beginning

The morning dawned bright and clear, casting a golden glow over the city of Atlanta. Vanessa Thompson stood by her bedroom window, gazing out at the bustling streets below. Her heart was filled with a sense of anticipation and purpose. Today marked the culmination of her journey with the spirits of Kwanzaa—a journey that had transformed her understanding of herself, her heritage, and her potential.

As she prepared for the day, Vanessa reflected on the lessons she had learned. Each principle had imparted its wisdom, guiding her toward a deeper connection with her roots and a clearer vision for her future. Umoja had taught her the power of unity; Kujichagulia, the importance of self-determination; Ujima, the strength of collective work; Ujamaa, the value of cooperative economics; Nia, the clarity of purpose; Kuumba, the inspiration of creativity; and Imani, the sustaining power of faith.

With these principles as her foundation, Vanessa felt ready to take bold steps forward. She envisioned TechSphere Innovations as a company that not only thrived in the tech industry but also served as a beacon of cultural empowerment and community engagement.

Later that morning, Vanessa arrived at her office with a renewed sense of determination. Her team had gathered for a special meeting, eager to hear her plans for the future. As she stood before them, Vanessa felt a surge of confidence and excitement. She was ready to share her vision and inspire others to join her on this transformative journey.

"Thank you all for being here today," Vanessa began, her voice steady and filled with passion. "Over the past few weeks, I've embarked on a journey of self-discovery and reflection. I've reconnected with the values that define who I am and what I want this company to stand for."

Her team listened intently, sensing the gravity of the moment. They had always admired Vanessa's leadership and drive, but today felt different—today, Vanessa was speaking from a place of deep conviction and purpose.

"I believe that TechSphere Innovations can be more than just a tech company," Vanessa continued. "We have the opportunity to be a force for good, to uplift our community and celebrate our cultural heritage through innovation."

She outlined her plans for new initiatives, including partnerships with local schools to support STEM education, collaborations with artists to create culturally-inspired tech projects, and community workshops that empowered aspiring entrepreneurs.

Her team responded with enthusiasm, their excitement palpable. They were inspired by Vanessa's vision and eager to contribute to a mission that resonated with their own values and aspirations.

As the meeting concluded, Vanessa felt a deep sense of fulfillment. She had taken the first step toward realizing her vision, and she knew that with the support of her team and community, they could achieve great things together.

In the weeks that followed, Vanessa worked tirelessly to implement her plans. She forged partnerships with local organizations, secured funding for community projects, and launched a series of innovative initiatives that celebrated African American culture and history.

The impact was immediate and profound. TechSphere Innovations became a hub of creativity and collaboration, attracting talent from diverse backgrounds and fostering a culture of inclusion and empowerment. The company's projects gained recognition for their ingenuity and social impact, positioning TechSphere as a leader in the tech industry and a champion of cultural empowerment.

Vanessa's journey had come full circle. She had embraced the teachings of the spirits and integrated them into every aspect of her life and work. Her legacy was one of unity, creativity, and purpose—a testament to the power of embracing one's heritage and using it as a foundation for growth and innovation.

As Vanessa stood on the rooftop of her office building, gazing out at the city that had inspired her journey, she felt a profound sense of gratitude. She had learned to trust in her vision, to lead with purpose, and to create a future that honored her past. With the principles of Kwanzaa as her guide, Vanessa was ready to continue her journey, confident in the knowledge that she was making a difference in the world.

The spirits had shown her the way, but it was Vanessa's courage, determination, and faith that had brought her vision to life. She knew that the journey was far from over—that there were new challenges to face and new opportunities to explore. But with the lessons of the past and the promise of the future, Vanessa was ready to embrace whatever lay ahead, confident in the knowledge that she was living a life of purpose, creativity, and community.

And so, with the city's lights twinkling in the distance and the stars shining brightly above, Vanessa Thompson stepped forward into a new beginning, her heart full of hope and her spirit guided by the timeless principles of her heritage.

Books by Kerry Brackett

Poetry

Soul Appetizer https://shorturl.at/cLFCn

An Open Table https://shorturl.at/SPjJy

Surviving Myself https://shorturl.at/U6eU1

Journeys of the Unseen series https://shorturl.at/8wqlz

    Shadows at Sundown

    Echoes of the Past

    Light on the Horizon

ABOUT THE AUTHOR

Kerry Brackett received his Ed.D. in Higher Education Administration from Liberty University and his MA in English and Creative Writing from Southern New Hampshire University. He has won a National Poetry Award for Freedom Poet of the Year in 2015 and a Gifted Artist Neo-Soul and Poetry Award in 2016. His poems, short stories, and essays appear or are forthcoming in many journals and anthologies, including *The Black & Latinx Poetry Project, The Griot, Simply Elevate Magazine, Spoken Vizions Magazine, Inner Child Press' I Want My Poetry to... Anthology* and *Wicked Shadow Press*. His debut poetry chapbook, *Soul Appetizer,* was self-published in 2012. His second book, *An Open Table*, was released in 2013. He released his third poetry chapbook, *Surviving Myself* (Guerrilla Ignition Publishing), in 2020. He had released numerous spoken word albums, including *Kadence of a Poetic Gentleman*, which won an Akademia Music Award for Best Spoken Word Album in 2016. His debut novel *Shadows at Sundown* was released in 2024. He currently lives in Bessemer, Alabama.